Rainbow Rider

Rainbow Rider

JANE YOLEN

Pictures by Michael Foreman

THOMAS Y. CROWELL COMPANY / NEW YORK

OTHER BOOKS BY JANE YOLEN:

The Bird of Time
The Boy Who Had Wings
The Girl Who Cried Flowers and Other Tales
The Girl Who Loved the Wind
The Wizard Islands

ISBN 0-690-00301-3

0-690-00311-0 (LB)

Library of Congress Cataloging in Publication Data   Yolen,
Jane H   Rainbow Rider.   SUMMARY: Saddened to dis-
cover that sand, tumbleweed and cactus are not suitable
friends, the Rainbow Rider flings his tears to the sky, and something special happens.   [1. Friendship—Fiction] I. Foreman,
Michael, 1938-   illus. II. Title. PZ7.Y78Rai [E] 73-
19700 ISBN 0-690-00301-3 ISBN 0-690-00311-0 (lib. bdg.)

1   2   3   4   5   6   7   8   9   10

Heidi heard it first,
Heidi loves it best.
This one is for Heidi.

In the time before time, the Rainbow Rider lived near
the edge of the desert by the foot of the painted hills.

He was the one who caught the drops of water that occasionally spilled from the desert sky. He was the one who bent them in an arch like his mighty hunting bow. Then he would fling the arch, shimmering and shining, back to the sky where it hung from one end of the earth to the other.

So he was the rainbow maker first.

But afterward, when he saw the great arch bending across the sky, he would jump on it and ride into Glory. And singing all the way.

Time in and time out, the Rainbow Rider made the arch. And time in and time out, he sang as he rode back and forth to Glory.

Yet at last he grew weary. And as he grew weary, he grew lonely.

So it came to pass that one time, in that time before time, the Rainbow Rider thought to himself, "I'll make me a friend."

But he had never made a friend before, and he was not sure how to begin. So he sat down by the edge of the desert by the foot of the painted hills. He took some sand while he thought, and trickled it through his fingers, just to pass away the time.

As the sand twinkled down, it made a pile. The pile grew big and the pile grew wide. It made the Rainbow Rider think.

"I can make my friend of sand," he thought.

And he did.

He pushed and he molded and he patted and he shaped until at last there stood a Sand Friend by his side.

"Welcome friend," said the Rainbow Rider, and he stuck out his hand.

But his hand poked right through the Sand Friend's chest. And the sand collapsed in a sparkling mound.

It made the Rainbow Rider cry.

And the time came in and the time went out and soon it was another time.

Sand didn't work. What should he try next?

The Rainbow Rider arose with the sun and cast his eyes up the desert and down. Pretty soon, he saw something coming toward him, tumbling in front of the wind. It came more than halfway to him when it stopped for the wind to catch its breath.

"I can't make me a friend of sand," thought the Rainbow Rider. "But I *can* make me a Tumbleweed Friend."

And he did.

He walked toward the weed and it tumbled toward him. And in the eyes of his mind, the Rainbow Rider could see a face beginning to grow on the tumbleweed. Two eyes so, and a nose so, and a mouth just starting to grin.

"Welcome friend," the Rainbow Rider called, and he stuck out his hand.

But just then the wind gave a mighty whoop, and the tumbleweed sped by his outstretched hand with not so much as a "How-de-do." And before the Rainbow Rider had time to call it back again. the Tumbleweed Friend had tumbled far and away down the desert sands and out of sight.

It made the Rainbow Rider cry.

And the time came in and the time went out and soon it was another time.

Sand didn't work. Tumbleweed didn't work. What should he try next?

The Rainbow Rider arose with the sun and cast his eyes up the desert and down. At last he stopped looking between the brown earth and the brown rocks and settled on a green cactus growing prickly in the sand.

"I can't make me a friend out of sand. And I can't make one of tumbleweed. But I can make me a Cactus Friend," he thought.

And he did.

The Rainbow Rider walked up to the cactus and set a desert flower on top.

"That for a hat," he said.

He found two black rocks for eyes. A thorn made a straight, thin nose. And a twig stuck tight to that thorny face made a mouth. Then he stood back to look and he liked what he saw.

"Welcome friend," said the Rainbow Rider, and he stuck out his hand.

The cactus did not move toward him, so the Rainbow Rider walked up close and tried again.

This time his hand got pricked on the cactus spines.

And what good is a friend who hurts you and can't come at least halfway to where you are?

So the Rainbow Rider cried again.

Sand didn't work. Tumbleweed didn't work. Cactus didn't work. And it didn't look like there was anything else to try next. Nothing but tears of his own, falling onto the Rainbow Rider's hands like rain from the desert skies.

Without thinking, the Rainbow Rider caught his own tears, as he had the rain, and bent them in an arch like his mighty hunting bow.

And then, just because he had that shimmering, shining arch and nothing better to do, he flung it to the sky where it hung from one end of the earth to the other.

Then he leaped onto the rainbow and rode off, once again, into Glory.

But this time, because he had made the arch of his own bright tears, Glory was different.

There was someone waiting at the rainbow's end.

Someone who moved toward him with a hand outstretched.

Someone who said, "Welcome friend."

And that was the time it all finally began.

JANE YOLEN is the author of many distinguished books for children, including *The Girl Who Cried Flowers*, *The Boy Who Had Wings*, *The Girl Who Loved the Wind*, *The Wizard Islands*, and *The Bird of Time*. Many of her original stories have a flavor of traditional folktales and, like them, are multileveled and can be enjoyed by adults as well as children. A graduate of Smith College, she worked for a time as a children's book editor for a New York publisher, but retired to devote her time to writing and teaching. With her husband and their three young children, Jane Yolen now lives in a lovely old farmhouse in Hatfield, Massachusetts.

MICHAEL FOREMAN is the internationally known author and illustrator of a growing list of distinguished picture books, including *War and Peas* and *Dinosaurs and All That Rubbish*. Winner of the Francis Williams Memorial Prize for his outstanding work in the graphic arts, he works as an illustrator and art director for magazines in the United States, Great Britain, and Europe. His work has taken him all over the world, even to Siberia and China. He has spent much time in the American west, and the Arizona landscape was the inspiration for his illustrations for *Rainbow Rider*. When not traveling, Mr. Foreman lives in London.